W9-ATN-429

Midway Middle School Media Center
425 Edgewater Drive
Midway, GA 31320

A Doctor
Like Papa

A Doctor Like Papa

by **NATALIE KINSEY-WARNOCK**
illustrated by James Bernardin

HarperCollins*Publishers*

A Doctor Like Papa

Text copyright © 2002 by Natalie Kinsey-Warnock

Illustrations copyright © 2002 by James Bernardin

All rights reserved. No part of this book may be used or reproduced
in any manner whatsoever without written permission except in the
case of brief quotations embodied in critical articles and reviews.
Printed in the United States of America. For information address
HarperCollins Children's Books, a division of HarperCollins
Publishers, 1350 Avenue of the Americas, New York, NY 10019.

www.harperchildrens.com

Library of Congress Cataloging-in-Publication Data

Kinsey-Warnock, Natalie.

A doctor like Papa / by Natalie Kinsey-Warnock ; illustrated by
James Bernardin.

    p.   cm.

Summary: When the influenza epidemic of 1918 comes to
Vermont, eleven-year-old Margaret, who has always wanted to be a
physician, finds out what doctoring is like.

ISBN 0-06-029319-5 — ISBN 0-06-029320-9 (lib. bdg.)

[1. Physicians—Fiction. 2. Sex role—Fiction. 3. Influenza—
Fiction. 4. Epidemics—Fiction. 5. Vermont—Fiction.]

I. Bernardin, James, ill. II. Title.

PZ7.K6293 Do   2002   2001039817

[Fic]—dc21   CIP

                                                      AC

Typography by Larissa Lawrynenko

1 2 3 4 5 6 7 8 9 10

First Edition

For Hannah

1

SOME EVENINGS, after supper, all of the family—Papa, Mama, Uncle Owen, Margaret, and Colin—sit on the porch and listen to the tree frogs trilling into the soft spring air and breathe in the smell of apple blossoms that have just come into bloom. Margaret leans against Uncle Owen and watches for the first star to wink out of the twilight. Then she squeezes her eyes shut and makes three wishes: one, for a sister; two, for a dog; and three, that Mama will change her mind about Margaret studying medicine. The third wish is the hardest. Margaret's never known Mama to change her mind about anything. "She's as stubborn as the day is long," Papa says fondly, but then he says the same thing about Margaret.

Sometimes, on those soft spring evenings, if Papa isn't too tired from his doctoring rounds, he'll take Mama's hand and they'll dance under the trees, and Papa sings softly, "I'll Be With You in Apple Blossom Time." On nights like this, it seems to Margaret that there is nothing in the whole wide world that can touch them.

But then, she is young and does not yet know about the war that is fixing to change their lives forever.

Before he left for the war in France, Uncle Owen planted an apple tree for Mama.

"I'm trusting you to take care of this tree," he said to Margaret. "Water it every week, and someday, when I get back, we'll pick apples together."

"Will you be gone a long time?" Margaret asked him.

"I might be," Uncle Owen said slowly.

He walked Margaret through the orchard,

telling her the names of the apples: Duchess, Astrachan, Bethel, Tetofsky, and Pound Sweet. He'd told them to her lots of times before, and she knew them all by heart, but she didn't mind hearing them again. Margaret knew it was going to be a while before she got to walk with Uncle Owen again, or hear his voice. She would miss Uncle Owen something awful. He seemed more like a brother to her than an uncle. He always listened to her, and he knew her three wishes.

As far back as she could remember, Margaret had wanted to be a doctor, just like Papa.

"Doctoring's no kind of life for a woman," Mama said. "It's too hard and dangerous."

Papa was the only doctor in the Northeast Kingdom of Vermont. He worked long hours and got called out in all kinds of weather. Being a doctor was a hard life, especially in the Kingdom, where roads were poor, people lived miles from one another, and winter lasted seven months a year. Sometimes, in blizzards, Papa snowshoed to patients, and once, in spring floods, he'd built a raft to get to people who needed him. But Margaret was sure it was just the life she wanted.

"She'll change her mind as she gets older," Mama said to Papa.

Margaret read her papa's medical books, even the parts she didn't understand. She begged and begged to ride with Papa on his house calls, but Mama wouldn't let her go.

"Margaret will make a good doctor," Uncle Owen had said.

"You shouldn't encourage her," Mama had scolded him. "It would be too hard a life for a woman. Maybe she could marry a doctor, like I did."

"No, Mama, I want to be a doctor myself," Margaret had said. Sometimes Mama was so old-fashioned, but Margaret was proud of her mama, too. Mama and Uncle Owen's ma and pa had gotten killed in a train wreck when Mama was only twelve. Mama had raised Uncle Owen and provided for them both. Margaret wondered how Mama had done it. She was almost twelve, too, and couldn't imagine losing Papa and Mama and having to raise up Colin all by herself.

Papa said he'd drive Uncle Owen to the train station. But Uncle Owen said, "Thank ye kindly, Reece, but I'd as lief walk." He waved good-bye, and Mama cried into her apron.

2

PAPA SAID it was a good thing they had a lot of work to do; it would help keep their minds off fretting over Uncle Owen. First they picked apples and made cider. Papa let Margaret climb the trees to shake the apples down. Colin ran under the trees. An apple plunked him on the head and he hollered.

"Get out of the way, then," Margaret hollered back. Colin was always in the way. For the hundredth time, Margaret wished she had a dog, or at least a sister, instead of a brother.

She and Colin helped dig the potatoes, carrots, turnips, and beets. Mama canned two hundred quart jars of vegetables and pickles.

"It's a comfort having a well-stocked pantry with winter coming," Mama said cheerfully. Lately Mama had talked a lot in her cheerful voice, ever since Uncle Owen had left. But Margaret wasn't fooled. Worry was written all over Mama's face, plain as day.

Papa hung the storm windows, and Margaret helped bank the house with fir boughs to keep out the cold winter winds. Together they wrapped burlap and wire around the trunk of the little apple tree to protect it from mice that burrowed under the snow and chewed young trees' tender bark.

Almost every week a letter came from Uncle Owen. Sometimes he wrote about bombed out villages, fields of trenches and barbed wire and the deadly gas used by the Germans, but he wrote, too, about places still untouched by war.

"The farmers are tilling their fields for next spring. They hitch their horses one ahead of the other instead of side by side. We caught a goose for Thanksgiving and had it with potatoes. We've had lots of apples since we came here. I should like to bring home some of the different kinds and plant them in our orchard. If I return from here, I think

I'd like to be a farmer and raise apples. I know I want no more of being a soldier."

And then, because soldiers weren't allowed to tell where they were, he closed his letters with "Somewhere in France."

Sometimes, after she read his letters, Mama got out her photo album and showed Margaret and Colin pictures of her ma and pa and told them stories of the apple orchard where she and Uncle Owen had played.

"We were allowed to climb all the trees except one," Mama said. "That was the one Great-grandfather had brought from Scotland. It was called a Stirling Castle, and it was such an old tree that Ma was afraid we'd break its branches. I'd love to taste one of those apples again."

Mama taught Margaret how to knit, and Margaret worked making a pair of socks for Uncle Owen. One sock was bigger than the other, but Mama said they would keep him warm, and she knit him a red scarf and green mittens.

Margaret longed to go with Papa on his rounds, but she knew Mama was so worried about Uncle Owen that she didn't beg. Instead, she helped Mama bake for Christmas. President Wilson had asked all Americans to eat less flour, sugar, eggs, and meat so that more could go to feed the soldiers. Mama made cakes and cookies that used no flour or eggs, and she used maple syrup for sweetening.

Even with Christmas coming, the household seemed sad and empty to Margaret. Always before, Uncle Owen had been there, singing Christmas carols and taking Margaret for rides in the sleigh. Mama played over and over on the Victrola the song "Keep the Home Fires Burning" and the record that sang of "peace on earth, goodwill toward men."

When Margaret thought of the war, she couldn't imagine Uncle Owen ever shooting at someone. Uncle Owen had never seemed much like a soldier. He never wanted to hurt anything and was happiest when he was digging in the soil and planting apple trees.

There had never been a winter such as the winter of 1918. The temperature dropped to forty below zero and hung there for days. But people still needed doctoring, so Papa had to go out in that cold weather and travel all over the county. Even wrapped in buffalo robes and wearing his heaviest woolen clothing, Papa would arrive home with his nose and ears turned white, and he wouldn't have any feeling in his fingers or toes. Margaret helped Mama rub snow on his hands and feet.

"One of these days you're going to freeze to death out there," Mama scolded. "You should stay home until this cold snap is over."

"I have to go, Edith," Papa said. "Folks don't stop getting sick or having babies just because the weather's cold."

Mama wouldn't let Margaret or Colin play outside. At night, even with four quilts piled on top of her, Margaret shivered in her bed, so Papa moved her and Colin into the kitchen. Mama closed off the rest of the rooms, and they ate and slept around the wood stove.

Margaret had never been so happy to see spring come. The long icicles on the roof melted. The brook swelled with melting snow and overflowed its banks. The woods began ringing with the *peent-peent* of woodcocks, the drumming of grouse, and the trilling of tree frogs. Margaret picked a bouquet of pussy willows for Mama.

If only Uncle Owen were home, everything would be perfect, she thought.

Papa cleaned the ashes out of the wood stove and took them to the orchard to sweeten the soil around the trees.

"That cold spell must have been too hard on the trees," he said when he returned. "Most of them are dead."

Margaret rushed to the orchard. The tree Uncle Owen had planted was bare and lifeless. How was she going to tell him she'd let the tree die? Uncle Owen had counted on her.

3

A T SCHOOL Miss Crawford surprised the students with an announcement.

"To celebrate Decoration Day this year, we're going to have a Historical Night," she said. "Each of you will choose a famous person to represent. You'll dress up as that person and say a little piece about him or her."

Right off, George Mooney picked George Washington.

"That way, I won't have to remember a different first name," he said, and Margaret hid a smile. Learning came hard to George; he'd had to repeat first and third grades, and this was his second year in the fifth grade. He was the oldest and biggest kid in class, and the only fifth grader who shaved.

Miss Crawford had to help some of the younger children choose their historical person, but by afternoon everyone had decided. Sally Rodgers picked Betsy Ross, Fred Chamberlain wanted to be Daniel Boone, and Mabel Waters chose Clara Barton.

"And whom shall you be, Margaret?" Miss Crawford asked.

"Elizabeth Blackwell," Margaret said.

"Who's that?" George asked.

"She was the first woman doctor," Margaret said.

When she told Papa and Mama her choice, Mama sighed.

"You couldn't be someone like Clara Barton or Florence Nightingale?" she said. "They were famous nurses."

"Mabel already picked Clara Barton, and besides, I don't want to be a nurse. I'm going to be a doctor."

"Elizabeth Blackwell's an admirable choice," Papa said. "Let's be more encouraging to Margaret."

"Why, Reece," Mama said. "I encourage Margaret."

"No, you don't," Margaret said softly. "You only tell me the things I can't do."

Mama looked hurt.

"I had no idea you thought that of me," Mama said. "I only want what's best for you."

"I know, Mama." Margaret sighed. She wondered if Mama would ever understand.

Friday night found everyone in town crowded into the schoolhouse. Miss Crawford had hung curtains around her desk to make it look like a stage. As each child stood on the desk to recite, Margaret hid in the curtains saying her piece over and over to herself and getting more nervous. She hoped she wouldn't forget what to say like George Mooney had.

Then it was Margaret's turn. She'd put on one of Mama's old dresses, and Mama had pinned up Margaret's hair so she'd look older. Papa had lent her his doctor's bag.

Margaret took a deep breath.

"Elizabeth Blackwell was the first woman doctor in the United States. Everyone told her

women couldn't be doctors, but she didn't listen."

Margaret found her mother's face in the crowd, and Mama gave her an encouraging smile.

"I've always wanted to be a doctor like Elizabeth Blackwell. My papa says she was a strong and brave woman, but there's somebody I think was even stronger and braver than Elizabeth Blackwell. My mama."

Mama's mouth formed an *O,* and Margaret hurried on.

"When my mama was twelve years old, her ma and pa got killed in a train wreck, and my mama had to raise Uncle Owen all by herself. I'm sure there were folks who thought she was too young to provide for them both, but she did it, and she did a good job, and even though I want to be a doctor, I hope I'm as strong and brave as my mama."

Mama dabbed at her eyes with a handkerchief. Papa beamed, and the audience burst into applause. Margaret sat down quickly.

"I wish Owen could have been here," Mama said as they all rode home in the buggy. "He'd be very proud of you." She was quiet for another mile, and Margaret knew she was thinking of Uncle Owen.

They pulled into the yard.

"I'll press your blue dress tonight, Margaret," Mama said, "so it'll be right ready for you in the morning. I want you to look your best when you go with Papa on his rounds."

Margaret stared at her in astonishment, and Papa grinned.

Mama gave him a stern look.

"Don't you grin at me, Reece McKenzie. I'm hoping she'll see doctoring isn't what she wants to do. I don't want life to be as hard for her as it was for Owen and me."

"It won't be," Papa said. "She'll have us."

Margaret wrapped her arms around Mama's waist and squeezed her hard.

"Thank you, Mama."

"Off to bed with you," Mama said. "I don't want to have to call you twice in the morning."

"You won't, Mama," Margaret said. "I promise."

4

THE HORSE'S HOOVES clip-clopped on the dirt road. Margaret sat straight and proud beside Papa, holding his doctor's bag on her lap. Papa had shown her all the things he carried in his bag—needles to give shots and needles to sew stitches, scalpels and bandages, pills and a shiny stethoscope. Papa had put the earpieces into Margaret's ears and placed the stethoscope on his chest. Margaret heard his strong heart beating.

Their first stop was at the Matthewses' farm.

"I see you've brought along an assistant," Mrs. Matthews said, and handed Margaret an oatmeal cookie warm from the oven.

"Thank you," said Margaret.

"What seems to be the trouble, Mrs. Matthews?" Papa asked.

"It's Edith," Mrs. Matthews said. "She's had a high fever since yesterday."

"Let's take a look," Papa said. "Margaret, you'd better wait out here. It might be contagious."

Margaret didn't want to wait outside. She wanted to help Papa. While she waited, she fed the horse some apples that had fallen in the Matthewses' orchard. It seemed a long time before Papa and Mrs. Matthews came back.

"It's scarlet fever," Papa said soberly. "She must stay in bed for six weeks." Margaret couldn't imagine staying in bed for six weeks. Now she was glad she hadn't gone inside. She didn't want to get scarlet fever.

"Feed Edith only milk and cereals," Papa said. "Nothing else until she's well."

"One thing we have on a farm is milk," Mrs. Matthews said. She set a fresh loaf of bread in the buggy.

"Why, that'll go good with supper," Papa said, pleased, but Margaret knew what Mama would say. She didn't like the way folks in the Kingdom paid Papa.

When Papa delivered Mrs. Bartholomew's baby, Mr. Bartholomew gave Papa three chickens. When Papa set Marcel LaBounty's broken leg, Marcel's mother handed Papa a sack of potatoes, and when Papa stitched up a deep cut on Cleon Jamison's head, Cleon sent along a gallon of maple syrup.

"I wish more of your patients paid you with real money," Mama said.

"Now, Edith," Papa said. "We're getting by all right. And we sure eat well. That's more than some can say. You know folks around here don't have much money."

"I know," said Mama. "But we can't pay our taxes with chickens."

Papa and Margaret's next stop was at the Atherton place. Mrs. Atherton met them in the yard.

"Clyde's got a terrible bellyache, Dr. McKenzie,"

Mrs. Atherton said, wringing her hands. "I'm afraid it's appendicitis."

Clyde rolled back and forth on his bed.

"I'm dying, I'm dying!" he moaned.

"It's appendicitis, isn't it?" Mrs. Atherton wailed. "Oh, I just know that's what it is. It killed my husband a few years back and now it's going to take my sweet boy!"

Papa was trying to examine Clyde.

"Hold still a minute," he said, but Clyde wouldn't hold still.

Something crunched under Margaret's shoe. She moved her foot and saw what looked like a small stone. She squatted to look. There were more of the stones under the bed. They looked like plum pits. From where she crouched, she could see one of Clyde's hands clutching the edge of the bed. His fingertips were stained purple.

Margaret tugged at Papa's coat.

"Papa," she whispered. "I think Clyde's got a stomachache from eating too many plums."

Mrs. Atherton heard Margaret and stopped wailing. She scowled at her son.

"Clyde Atherton, have you been into my plums again? I'll tan your hide, boy."

Papa's eyes were laughing.

"Now, Mrs. Atherton, you wait till he's better before you paddle him."

5

PAPA CLUCKED to the horse, and off they went. He was still chuckling about Clyde when a girl ran in front of the buggy. The horse reared, and Margaret was sure she and Pa were going to be crushed.

"Why, Edith," Papa said. "What's wrong?"

"Oh, Dr. McKenzie! Come quick!" the girl said. "Pa's near cut his foot off!"

Margaret had never seen so much blood. She felt a little sick, but she wanted Papa to be proud of her. She made herself smile at the man.

"You'll be all right," she told him. "My papa will fix you up as good as new."

Papa gave the man chloroform to make him

sleep, and Margaret watched him stitch the muscles and tendons and skin back together. She handed Papa scissors when he asked for them, and she helped bandage the foot from toes to knee.

"That girl's got a knack for doctoring," the man's wife said.

"Yes, she does," Papa said proudly.

"Well, she'll have some big shoes to fill," the woman said. "We're lucky to have such a fine doctor as you." Margaret was proud that the people of the Kingdom loved her papa so.

While Papa was cleaning up at the washbasin, the woman called to her daughter.

"Go get Dr. McKenzie a cool drink from the well." Edith brought Margaret a glass of water, too.

"Are you really going to be a doctor?" Edith asked.

"Yes, I am," Margaret said.

Edith looked at her with big eyes.

"I didn't know girls could be doctors," she said.

"You handled yourself well back there, Margaret," Papa said as they drove on.

In the afternoon, Margaret helped Papa set a

broken arm, pull a tooth, and even treat a horse for colic. She met two more girls named Edith.

Margaret wondered why so many girls in the Kingdom were named Edith. She was about to ask Papa when Mr. Cowan flagged them down.

"Dr. McKenzie, Sarah's having her baby!"

At the Cowans', Papa made Margaret wait in the kitchen with Mr. Cowan and his five sons. Not one of them said a word.

Every time Mrs. Cowan hollered, Mr. Cowan and his sons jumped. Margaret jumped, too. Papa seemed to be taking an awfully long time.

It was almost dark when Papa walked out of the bedroom.

"It's a girl," he said.

"A girl!" Mr. Cowan whooped in delight. "We were sure it'd be another boy. We don't even have a girl's name picked out. Any suggestions, Doc?"

"Well," said Papa, "Edith's a nice name." Margaret almost laughed out loud. That's why there were so many Ediths in the Kingdom. Papa was naming them after Mama!

She was still smiling when she and Papa walked into the kitchen, still smiling until she saw

the envelope in Mama's hand. Mama's face was as white as bone.

"This telegram came today," Mama said. "Oh, Reece, I was too afraid to open it."

Papa read the telegram and wrapped his arms around Mama.

"Is he dead?" Mama whispered.

"I don't know," he said. "The telegram says he's missing."

6

MARGARET TUCKED Colin into bed without being told. For once, Colin didn't argue about going to bed.

"Is Uncle Owen lost?" Colin asked.

"I guess so," Margaret said. She didn't really know what missing meant either.

Papa came in to say good night.

"Why is Mama crying?" Colin asked.

"She's afraid for Uncle Owen," Papa said. "She's always watched over him just like Margaret watches over you."

"I don't need anyone to watch over me," Colin said hotly.

Papa laughed and Margaret smiled. Sometimes

Colin made her so mad, but she was glad he'd made Papa laugh. There'd been too much sadness since Uncle Owen left.

The summer passed with no word of Uncle Owen. Mama got thin, and there were dark circles under her eyes. Margaret worried about her.

Margaret still went on calls with Papa, but whenever she and Papa were home, she tried to keep Colin from bothering Mama. She took him fishing, played hide-and-seek, and built forts. They were playing cowboys and Indians one day in the orchard when Colin announced, "Somebody's coming."

A boy was pushing a bicycle up the hill. When he got closer, Margaret was surprised to see it was George Mooney. He arrived in the yard out of breath and pulled an envelope from his pocket.

"Telegram," he said. When Margaret made no move to take it, George pushed it into her hands.

"I got me a job," he said proudly. "Delivering telegrams for the telegraph office. I ain't gonna go back to school no more. Pa says I don't have to."

Margaret stared at the envelope in her hands. It looked just like the one Mama had gotten telling that Uncle Owen was missing.

"Maybe it's good news," she said slowly.

"Naw," George said, swinging his leg over the seat for the ride back down into town. "I ain't seen a telegram yet that had good news."

The color drained from Mama's face when she saw the envelope in Margaret's hand. Papa reached for it, tore the envelope open, and scanned the contents.

"Owen's alive!" he said. He caught Mama in his arms and twirled her around the room.

"Where is he?" Mama asked. "When is he coming home?"

"He's been in a hospital in France," Papa said. "As soon as he can travel, they'll ship him home."

"He's hurt, then?" Mama said.

"Yes," Papa said. "He's lost an arm."

Mama covered her face.

"My poor Owen," she said.

"He's alive, Edith," Papa said gently.

"Yes," Mama said, wiping away tears. "That's what matters."

7

UNCLE OWEN came home at the end of August, but Margaret hardly recognized him. He looked old and shriveled. Margaret tried not to stare at the empty sleeve of his coat. When she hugged him, he didn't hug back. He didn't work in the orchard, or whistle, or tell stories to Margaret and Colin anymore. In fact, he didn't talk at all, and a dark room frightened him. He sat in his chair or lay on his bed with the lantern glowing all night, just staring up at the ceiling, as silent as the stars.

One night, after they'd eaten and Mama had carried supper in to Uncle Owen, Margaret and Papa sat together on the porch steps. Crickets

sawed away in the darkness, and overhead the Milky Way ran through the sky like a moonlit river. Margaret thought back to those other nights when the whole family had gathered on the porch, before Uncle Owen had gone for a soldier. It seemed like a million years ago.

"What's wrong with Uncle Owen?" Margaret asked Papa.

Papa thought awhile.

"You know, my pa was in the Civil War, and he came home a changed man, too. He had nightmares, would wake up screaming and then shake for hours. He started hearing voices, of his friends who hadn't made it home. War does that to a person. A soldier sees such terrible things that his brain goes into shock."

"Can't you do something for him?" Margaret asked. "To make him feel better?"

Papa shook his head.

"There are some things doctors can't fix," he said.

8

MARGARET AND COLIN went back to school, but Margaret missed going on rounds with Papa.

"Couldn't I just go with you?" she asked Papa. "Mr. Mooney let George quit school."

"Margaret, doctors need years of schooling," Papa said. "You have to get good grades to get into medical college, and because you're a woman, your grades will have to be perfect before they'll even consider you."

"That's not fair," Margaret said.

"No, it isn't," Papa said, "but that's the way things are."

So, every evening until she went to bed,

Margaret studied hard, and on Saturdays she went with Papa on his rounds. One Saturday in October, Papa was already gone when she got up.

"George Mooney fetched your papa during the night," Mama said. "Said his whole family's sick."

Noon came and went and Papa did not come home. All afternoon, Margaret listened for the sound of the buggy.

Finally, near dusk, she heard it and skipped out to meet Papa. She wondered why Papa had halted the horse in the orchard.

"Stay back, Margaret!" Papa shouted. "Don't come any closer!"

Margaret stood, wide eyed and frightened. Papa had never spoken to her like that.

Mama heard Papa shout, and she stepped out into the yard.

"What is it, Reece?" Mama called out. "What's wrong?"

"Mr. Mooney and one of his daughters died today, and now George has come down with it. Whatever it is they have, it's deadly, and I don't want to risk you and the children getting it, so I'm going to stay in Mooney's barn tonight. I'll stop by

in the morning to let you know what's happening."

Mama wasn't bustling around as she usually did on Sunday mornings, getting everyone dressed in their best clothes.

"Aren't we going to church?" Colin asked.

"Not this morning," Mama said. "We're going to wait till Papa comes by."

Margaret and Colin looked at each other. Mama never missed church.

They all heard Papa's buggy. This time Margaret knew better than to run out to him.

"How are Mrs. Mooney and the other children?" Mama called out.

Papa looked at her and shook his head. Mama caught her breath.

"All of them?" she asked quietly, and Papa nodded. Margaret looked at Mama's face, trying to understand. Did Papa mean that *all* the Mooneys had died?

"I've seen twenty more sick just this morning," Papa said. "It's some type of influenza, but much worse than any flu or pneumonia I've ever seen before. It seems to be spreading like wildfire. I won't be coming home till this is over. I'll swing by when I can, just to make sure you're all right. You've got enough flour, sugar, and tea to last a few weeks, if necessary?"

"Yes, Reece, we'll be fine," Mama said. "The pantry is well stocked. Just take care of yourself."

The days were long and lonely without Papa. Margaret watched for him at the window, and at night she listened for the buggy until she fell asleep.

It was a week before Papa stopped by again. Margaret couldn't believe how much Papa had changed. He was gaunt and hollow eyed.

"Reece, you'll be sick yourself," Mama scolded.

"There's so many sick, I can't take care of them all," Papa said. "I'm seeing a hundred patients a day, and I still can't get to everybody. If I come to a house and there's no smoke coming out of the chimney, I figure I'm too late and I drive on to the next place."

"Too late for what?" Colin whispered. Margaret shook her head.

"It's as bad as that?" Mama asked.

Papa rubbed his bloodshot eyes. "So many have died, the undertaker has run out of coffins," he said.

Margaret and Mama watched him drive off, and for the first time, Margaret realized he might not come home again.

9

MARGARET LAY AWAKE a long time. Papa was risking his life to help others. For the first time, Margaret wondered whether she really *did* want to be a doctor.

Margaret and Mama were surprised to hear the buggy again the very next morning. Clyde Atherton was in the buggy with Papa.

"Clyde's mother died about an hour ago, and he has no other family," Papa said. "I didn't know where else to take him."

Margaret remembered how Mrs. Atherton had been so afraid Clyde would die from appendicitis. Now she was the one who was dead.

Margaret stared at Clyde. He hadn't moved, or

said a word, since they'd pulled into the yard, just sat small and pale, staring straight ahead at nothing in particular. Just like Uncle Owen.

"The poor thing," Mama said. "You did right to bring him here, Reece. But what about the danger to Margaret and Colin?"

"I already called Aunt Clarissa from town," Papa said. "She said they can stay with her."

Aunt Clarissa lived by herself on a little farm on Dexter Mountain. Margaret liked visiting her, but she'd never been allowed to go there by herself. You had to go up and over three other hills to get there.

"You and Colin had best put on your warmest clothes," Mama said. "There's bound to be snow up in the hills."

Papa and Clyde stayed in the buggy while Mama saddled Nellie, Papa's other horse. Mama kissed Margaret on both her cheeks and set her on Nellie's back. She did the same with Colin, putting him in front of Margaret, where Margaret could hold on to him. Mama tucked bags of johnnycake and cheese into Margaret's coat pockets. Margaret blinked back tears. She saw Uncle Owen looking out the window and wished he was going along with her and Colin.

"How long will we have to stay with Aunt Clarissa?" Margaret asked.

"Until the influenza is over," Mama said. She looked like she was blinking back tears, too. "If Papa and I . . . if something happens . . . well, Aunt Clarissa will take care of you."

It wasn't so much her words that chilled Margaret. It was what Mama hadn't said. If Papa and I die. . . .

"Margaret, go straight to Aunt Clarissa's," Papa called out. "Don't stop anywhere along the way."

Margaret and Colin and Nellie crossed the fields and the brook and climbed the first hill. The trail was so overgrown that Margaret had to watch constantly to make sure she was headed the right way. When she did make a wrong turn, she got scared. What if she got lost? No one would know she and Colin were missing. Mama and Papa were counting on her.

Margaret backtracked and found the trail again. They climbed to where the trees were bent and stunted by the wind. Nellie's hooves made

prints in the snow, and when Margaret looked west at the line of the Green Mountains, she saw they had white tops, too.

The trail wound down into the valley again and became a maple-lined road, with fields on either side. They even passed a few apple trees that hadn't been killed by the winter's cold spell. The apples were crisp and juicy, and she and Colin munched on them as they rode along.

They climbed the second hill. At the top, Margaret paused a moment to drink in the view. The hills rolled on and on until they met the sky, like waves in a lake, and so much color: green fields and deep blue sky and the leaves that still clung to the trees were in every shade of red and orange and gold. If Margaret hadn't been so worried about Mama and Papa, she would have felt like singing.

"I'm hungry," Colin said, so Margaret pulled the bag from her pocket.

"Why do they call it johnnycake?" Colin asked, taking a big bite of the corn bread.

"Mama says it used to be called journey-cake," Margaret said. "I guess because you could take it with you on a journey."

"Like we're doing," Colin said. To him this all seemed like a great adventure. He was too young to understand the danger to Mama and Papa and Uncle Owen, but Margaret was afraid. What if they all died? She and Colin would be left alone, just as Mama and Uncle Owen had been. Colin would be her only family.

She hugged him hard.

"Ow!" Colin hollered "You're squishing my guts out." Margaret laughed. Sometimes she was glad he was her brother.

They climbed the third hill. There was snow on the ground, and the dark clouds threatened more. Margaret felt Colin shivering, and she hugged him again.

"We'll be to Aunt Clarissa's soon," she said. "She'll make us hot cocoa, and I bet her cookie jar is full of molasses crinkles." Molasses crinkles were her and Colin's favorite.

At first Margaret thought the sound was the wind, moaning as it swept over the tops of the hills, but then it rose above the wind, a low, unearthly howl that made the hairs on her neck stand up. Colin heard it, too.

"What was that?" he asked.

"I don't know," she said.

"I bet it's ghosts," Colin said. "Or werewolves."

"There's no such thing, either one," Margaret said, but she shivered, too.

The road branched, and Margaret hesitated.

"Which way is Aunt Clarissa's?" Colin asked.

"That way," Margaret said, pointing right. "But I think the sound came from the left."

"Let's not go there," Colin said. "I don't want to meet a werewolf."

"It wasn't a werewolf," Margaret said. "But it might have been a hurt animal. Maybe it's caught in a trap. We'll ride down here just a little ways, and if we don't find anything, we'll come back, okay?" She could tell Colin was scared, but he nodded, and she turned Nellie down the left-hand road.

Colin was trying hard to be brave, but he jumped at every sound. "Can we go now?" Colin asked. "I'm thirsty."

Margaret was thirsty, too. In all the rush, Mama had forgotten to send along a canteen of water.

Margaret saw a farmhouse coming into view.

"I see a farmhouse ahead," she said. "We'll turn around there and get a drink." Papa had said not to stop along the way, but it couldn't hurt just to get some water from their well.

They rode into the yard. A black-and-white border collie lay in the dirt, sleeping. A chain stretched from the dog's collar to the barn, and an empty dish lay beside it. The sight of that empty dish bothered Margaret. There was no telling how long the dog had been without food or water. If she had a dog, she wouldn't keep it chained and she'd take good care of it.

"Hello!" Margaret called out, as they rode into the yard. "Hello?"

No one answered. No one came to the door. Other than a few scrawny chickens in the yard, there wasn't a sign of life. Even the dog didn't raise its head, and Margaret realized it wasn't sleeping. It was dead.

Something Papa had said came to Margaret's mind. She raised her eyes to the roof.

There wasn't any smoke coming from the chimney.

A chill skipped up Margaret's spine.

"Margaret," Colin whispered. "I don't like it here."

"Me, neither," said Margaret. "Let's go." Nellie seemed eager to leave, too, and pranced toward the road, but not before Margaret saw the dog's tail sweep across the dirt.

Margaret scrambled off Nellie, dragging Colin with her.

"Take that dish and get some water at the pump," she told him. Margaret unhooked the chain and ran her fingers over the dog's ribs. Again, the tail wagged.

Colin came running back, water sloshing from the bowl. He set it beside the dog, but she didn't raise her head.

"She's too weak," Margaret said. She tore a piece from her shirt, dipped the cloth in the bowl, and dribbled water into the dog's mouth. Margaret waited for the dog to swallow, but nothing happened. Margaret lifted the dog's head in her lap. She dribbled more water down its throat and stroked its neck. She almost cheered when the dog swallowed.

Colin filled the bowl three more times, and Margaret trickled water down the dog's throat until, finally, it raised its head and lapped Margaret's hand. Margaret felt her eyes fill with tears. She'd always wanted a dog just like this one, but now her wish seemed selfish. She hadn't wanted a whole family to die just so she could get a dog. All her wishes seemed selfish now: a sister, a dog, and Mama to change her mind. All Margaret really wanted was for her family to be all right and for Uncle Owen to be the way he used to be.

"We'll take the dog to Aunt Clarissa's," Margaret said. She boosted Colin up into the saddle. It took all her strength to lift the dog, but with Colin pulling on its collar and Margaret pushing from below, they managed to get the dog draped across the saddle, too. Margaret climbed the rail fence to get on Nellie, and they headed down the road. Margaret knew they made an odd sight, but there was no one around to see them.

"Why didn't we go into the house?" Colin asked.

Margaret didn't want Colin to know that

everyone inside was dead.

"There wasn't anybody there," she said.

"I saw somebody," Colin said.

"What?" Margaret said. "What do you mean?"

"In the window," Colin said. "I saw a face."

10

MARGARET PULLED Nellie to a stop.

"A face? Are you sure?" she asked.

Colin nodded.

"A little girl," he said.

Margaret didn't know what to do. If she went back, she'd be putting herself and Colin in danger. But that little girl might be the only person alive in the house. Margaret couldn't just leave her.

She tried to think. What would Papa do?

Papa knew the influenza might kill him. But still he went wherever people needed him. To Papa, that's what being a doctor meant.

Margaret knew that's the kind of doctor she wanted to be, too.

Margaret led Nellie into the barn and pulled the collie off her back. She laid the dog in the hay, filled the bowl with water, and gave Nellie a bucket of water, too. Colin followed her around like a dog while she worked, and he wanted to go into the house with her.

"You can't, Colin," she said.

"Why not?"

"Because there's some sick people in the house, and you might catch it. You have to stay in the barn."

"All by myself?" Colin said. "It'll be dark out there."

"I know," Margaret said. "You'll have to be really brave, okay?" She could see Colin's lower lip trembling, but he nodded.

Margaret's hand trembled, too, as she opened the door.

It took a few moments for her eyes to adjust to the darkness inside, enough to see a woman's body on the floor. The house was so cold she could see her breath.

"Mama's sick," a voice said.

Margaret turned her head at the sound. A pale

shaft of sunlight was slanting through the window, and a little girl was sitting in the shaft, trying to get warm.

"I bet your name is Edith," Margaret said. The little girl's eyes grew round, and she nodded.

"I bet you're hungry, too," Margaret said, and Edith nodded again.

Edith's mother's skin was hot to touch, and her breath rattled in her chest. Again Margaret tried to think what Papa would do.

She carried in an armful of wood and got a fire roaring in the stove. She boiled kettles of water to fill the house with steam. Papa said that helped people breathe. She soaked towels in cold water and wrapped them around the woman's forehead and neck to bring down her fever. Papa said sick people needed fluids, too. Mama always said chicken soup was good for any ailment, so Margaret gritted her teeth and caught one of the chickens in the yard. She closed her eyes to wring its neck, and dressed it the way she'd seen Mama do. Soon she had a pot of chicken soup bubbling away on the stove. Edith gobbled down a bowl of the soup, then climbed into Margaret's lap and put

her thumb in her mouth. Margaret rocked her, singing softly until Edith fell asleep.

Margaret knelt beside the woman and spooned some broth into her mouth. The woman swallowed, and Margaret spooned in a little more. The woman opened her eyes once.

"Edith?" she whispered.

"She's right here," Margaret said. "She's all right." The woman closed her eyes again. Margaret sat back on her heels and realized how tired she was. She'd done everything she knew to do. She closed her eyes, too, and when she opened them again, it was dark outside. It was quiet, too, no sound of someone gasping for air. The woman wasn't breathing anymore.

A shudder passed through Margaret. She scooped up Edith, her heart pounding, and ran for the barn, startling Colin when she burst through the door. He'd been crying, Margaret could tell, by the dirty tear tracks down his face. She leaned against the door and tried to catch her breath.

"We're going to stay here with you," she said as cheerfully as she could. Colin seemed to know better than to ask why she wasn't staying in the house. He was just glad not to be alone.

"I wasn't scared, Margaret," he said. "But the dog was."

Margaret made herself smile at him.

"Well, she had nothing to be afraid of," Margaret said. "You were here." She was glad to see Colin's shoulders straighten with pride.

The four of them—Margaret, Colin, Edith, and the dog—curled up together in the hay with Nellie's saddle blanket over them. Margaret lay awake a long time, watching how the moonlight played on the rafters and trying not to think about Edith's mother. The dog gave a long sigh and laid its head on Margaret's arm.

"If you hadn't howled right when you did," Margaret said, "who knows how long it would have been before someone came by your place. Mama would say you'd been saved by the grace of God."

Margaret curled up against the dog and fell asleep listening to the *thump, thump, thump* of Grace's heart.

11

THE SOUND of the buggy woke her up.

Papa opened the door and Margaret ran into his arms.

"Aunt Clarissa called and said you never showed up," Papa said. "I've been hunting for you all night. When it got light enough to see, I found your tracks coming down this road. What made you come this way?"

Papa's voice had woken Colin, too, and he tackled Papa.

"We heard werewolves, Papa," Colin said.

"No, it was this dog," Margaret contradicted. "I heard her howl. She was trying to get help." Grace raised her head and wagged her tail.

"I tried to help, Papa," Margaret said, and told him the whole story. She cried when she got to the part about Edith's mother. "I tried to save her, but she died."

Papa wrapped his arms around her.

"I couldn't have done any better myself, Margaret," he said. "Doctors can't save everyone, and this influenza has made me feel pretty helpless, but we do the best we can, and then we go on to help someone else. At least Edith's mother didn't have to die alone in a cold, dark house, wondering if anyone would find her little girl."

Papa loaded them all in the buggy.

"I'm going to take a look in the house," he whispered to Margaret. "See if anyone else was there."

He was gone only a minute. He strode back toward them, his face grim. He saw the question in Margaret's eyes.

"The father and brother were in the back rooms," he said quietly.

Margaret shuddered. She was glad she hadn't known that.

When they came out of the last curve toward home, Margaret saw the orchard sweep into view, the barn sitting against the hill, and the sun rising over it, and her throat closed up. Then Mama came flying down the steps of the house to greet them, her smile flashing like heat lightning, and Margaret wanted to weep. She'd only been gone a day and night, but she felt years older, and Mama and home had never looked so beautiful.

Mama took one look at Edith and swooped her into her arms.

"You poor thing," she said. "You can't understand right now, but I know just how you feel."

Papa lifted Grace from the buggy and set her on the ground. She stood, swaying, looking around at her new home. Mama's eyes widened in surprise.

Margaret hadn't thought about whether Mama would let her keep Grace. Mama didn't care for dogs, but Margaret hoped she'd be able to convince Mama to let her keep Grace in the barn, at least until Grace got stronger. Margaret would sneak her out some food later.

"Why, she's starving," Mama said. "Margaret, get her some of the pork roast left over from supper. I suspect you could eat a little, too. I'm going to get this poor child into clean clothes and fix her a good hot meal."

Margaret was surprised to see Uncle Owen sitting on the porch. Clyde was curled up in his lap. They were both asleep.

"I think Owen's been a help to Clyde," Mama said to Papa. "They've both been through terrible ordeals, and Owen knows what it's like to lose both parents."

"I think Clyde will be a help to Owen," Papa said. "Nothing gets your mind off your own troubles faster than helping someone else get over theirs."

Margaret helped the dog up the porch steps. As they passed Uncle Owen, Grace nudged his hand. Uncle Owen started awake, making an awful moaning sound in his throat. Margaret had never seen such a look of terror on anyone's face. She grabbed Grace and pulled her away, but as soon as Uncle Owen saw Grace, his expression changed. He reached down to touch her. Margaret saw his hand was shaking. When he began talking, his voice sounded squeaky, like it had lain out too long in the rain and rusted.

"It was a Red Cross dog found me on the battlefield. She stayed right next to me, even with shells exploding over our heads. Then she brought a medic to me. I never saw her again after that."

Colin climbed right into Uncle Owen's lap, even though Clyde was already there, and pulled an apple from his coat pocket. Margaret saw it was one of the apples she'd picked while she and Colin were riding.

"I brought you a present," Colin said. "I know you like apples."

Uncle Owen looked at Colin like he didn't quite remember who he was. He rubbed the apple on his shirt and took a bite. A strange look came over his face.

"Edith, taste this," he said. Mama bit into it, too.

"Why, it's a Stirling Castle!" she said. "Just like the ones we had as children! Where'd you find it?"

"On the way to Aunt Clarissa's," Margaret said. "I'll show you, and in the spring, you could get branches off those trees and start a new orchard here."

"In the spring," Uncle Owen said slowly. "Yes, you can show me in the spring." He sat rocking Colin and Clyde in his lap, humming so softly that it took Margaret a moment before she recognized the tune. He was humming "I'll Be With You in Apple Blossom Time."

12

THE WAR ENDED on November 11, 1918. People cheered and hugged one another, and all night long the sound of bells could be heard ringing throughout the hills as towns celebrated.

Margaret was glad the war was over, but she couldn't help remembering how things had been before Uncle Owen went to war and before the influenza, when her life had seemed so safe.

In December Papa said what he wanted most for Christmas was a week of sleep. He did manage to spend Christmas Eve at home, so Christmas, if not merry, was at least made better because they were all together. Margaret's present was a gleaming new stethoscope.

"For you to take to medical college," Mama said.

"Oh, Mama, I don't want to be a doctor anymore," Margaret said. "You were right. It's too hard."

Instead of being happy, Mama got a fierce look in her eye. She gripped Margaret's shoulders so hard they hurt.

"No, I wasn't right," Mama said. "I only wanted to protect you, but I didn't do that. Being a doctor will be hard, but most worthwhile things in life are. You're going to be a wonderful doctor. Just like your papa."

The influenza left as mysteriously as it had arrived. There were no cases the last week in February, and Papa came home and slept for three days straight. But nothing would ever be the same.

School reopened, with a lot of the familiar faces gone: George Mooney, Mabel Waters, and Miss Crawford among them. Johnny Baker had gone to live with relatives in Connecticut, and Annabelle

LeBlanc was now living with a cousin in Quebec, but there were new faces, too. The Daniels family had taken in a niece from near Burlington way, and the Gosselin family had made room for an orphaned cousin from Montreal, families everywhere cobbled together by heartache.

Margaret was reminded every moment of every day how much her family had changed, but they were still a family, in spirit if not by blood. Clyde was as quiet as Uncle Owen, but Margaret could look out and see the two of them working together in the orchard or the garden, and know they were both better for having each other. And if Edith wasn't the sister Margaret had dreamed about, well, she was something very close to it.

Grace loved them all, but if Uncle Owen and Clyde went out to plant trees, Grace trotted beside them, or if they were sitting together on the porch, listening to tree frogs trill away the night, Grace was between them, and one, or both of them, would be stroking her head or scratching her behind the ears. It was as if she knew Uncle Owen and Clyde needed her more than Margaret did.

Margaret graduated medical college at the top of her class and began her practice in the Kingdom. She made her rounds in a Model A Ford instead of a buggy. The people of the Kingdom called her Dr. Margaret, even after she'd married, and came to love her as much as they did her father.

Sometimes she and Papa went on house calls together, just as they had when Margaret was young, but it was Mama who delivered Margaret's first child.

"What are you going to name your new daughter?" Papa asked.

"Well, Edith's a nice name," Margaret said, her eyes twinkling.

"Goodness," said Mama. "Haven't enough girls in the Kingdom been named Edith?" But Margaret could tell she was pleased, and Mama was only too happy to watch little Edith when Margaret went on her rounds. They went on walks, picked flowers, and baked cookies.

One morning Edith was missing. Mama, Papa, Uncle Owen, Margaret, and her husband, Tom, searched frantically and finally found her asleep in

the car with Margaret's doctor bag in her lap.

Margaret wondered what Mama would say, but Mama only smiled and shook her head.

"Here we go again," she said.

Author's Note

The 1918–1919 influenza epidemic killed more than 50 million people worldwide. It struck young and old alike, taking children from parents, parents from children. Doctors worked themselves to exhaustion trying to care for all the sick.

My mother remembers hearing Dr. Frank Easton of Craftsbury Common, Vermont, tell of having so many patients to treat that if there wasn't smoke coming from a chimney, he knew he was too late and drove on to the next house. He and his son had driven by one such place when his son saw a face in the window.* They went back and found a little girl sitting in the sunshine, trying to keep warm in a cold house. Her parents and brother were dead. She was one of the many orphans the flu epidemic created.

* from *As I Recall,* recollections of Dr. Frank Easton, compiled by his daughter, Paula Easton Stannard

Midway Middle
Media Center
Enamored
912-984-5841

Midway Middle School
Media Center
425 Edgewater Drive
Midway GA 31320
912-884-5843